Little Wolf and Smellybreff

Badness for Beginners

For Teddy and Ella –
who never get spoilt rotten, hem hem –
with love from You-Know-Who.

First published in paperback in Great Britain by HarperCollins Children's Books in 2005

1 3 5 7 9 10 8 6 4 2

ISBN: 978-0-00-783782-3

Text copyright Ian Whybrow © 2005
Illustrations copyright Tony Ross © 2005

HarperCollins Children's Books is a division of HarperCollins Publishers Ltd.

The author and illustrator assert the moral right to be identified
as the author and illustrator of the work.
A CIP catalogue record for this title is available from the British Library.
All rights reserved. No part of this publication may be reproduced, stored in a
retrieval system or transmitted in any form or by any means, electronic, mechanical, photocopying,
recording or otherwise, without the prior permission of HarperCollins Publishers Ltd,
77-85 Fulham Palace Road, Hammersmith, London W6 8JB.

Visit our website address at: www.harpercollinschildrensbooks.co.uk

Printed and bound in Malaysia

Little Wolf and Smellybreff
Badness for Beginners

Ian Whybrow + Tony Ross

HarperCollins *Children's Books*

In a nice smelly lair, far away, lived the Wolf family.
There was Mum Wolf, Dad Wolf, Little Wolf and
Baby Wolf. (He was the smelliest, so they
called him Smellybreff).

Mum and Dad were very proud of being big and bad.
They wanted Little and Smellybreff to grow
up big and bad like them.

Mum and Dad taught the cubs Naughty Nursery Rhymes.
Their favourite was "Never Say Thank You".

Never say thank you
Play with your food
Make all your noises
Naughty and rude
Talk with your mouth full
Answer back quick
Never stop eating
till you feel sick

Smellybreff was a quick learner; he was full of Badness.

But sometimes Little was good by mistake.

One day, Mum and Dad decided to teach Little and Smells
some more Badness lessons. Off they went to town.
"Remember," said Dad. "You must BOTH
be on your worst behaviour."

The Wolf family came to a bridge that was being mended.
Dad said, "Watch me!"

He went, "GURRR!" and scared the menders away.

He kicked over their Danger sign.

He kicked over their warning lights and he ate their sandwiches.

Mum said, "Well done, Dad! That was very nasty and horrible! What a fine example to the cubs!"

Smellybreff wanted to be nasty and horrible like his Dad. Little said, "No, Smells, you are only a baby. Watch me!"

He made a mud pie in the road. (It wasn't a very bad thing to do, but Little was trying his hardest.)

Smellybreff went screamy-scream.

Then he jumped on the menders' drill and went...

BRRRR

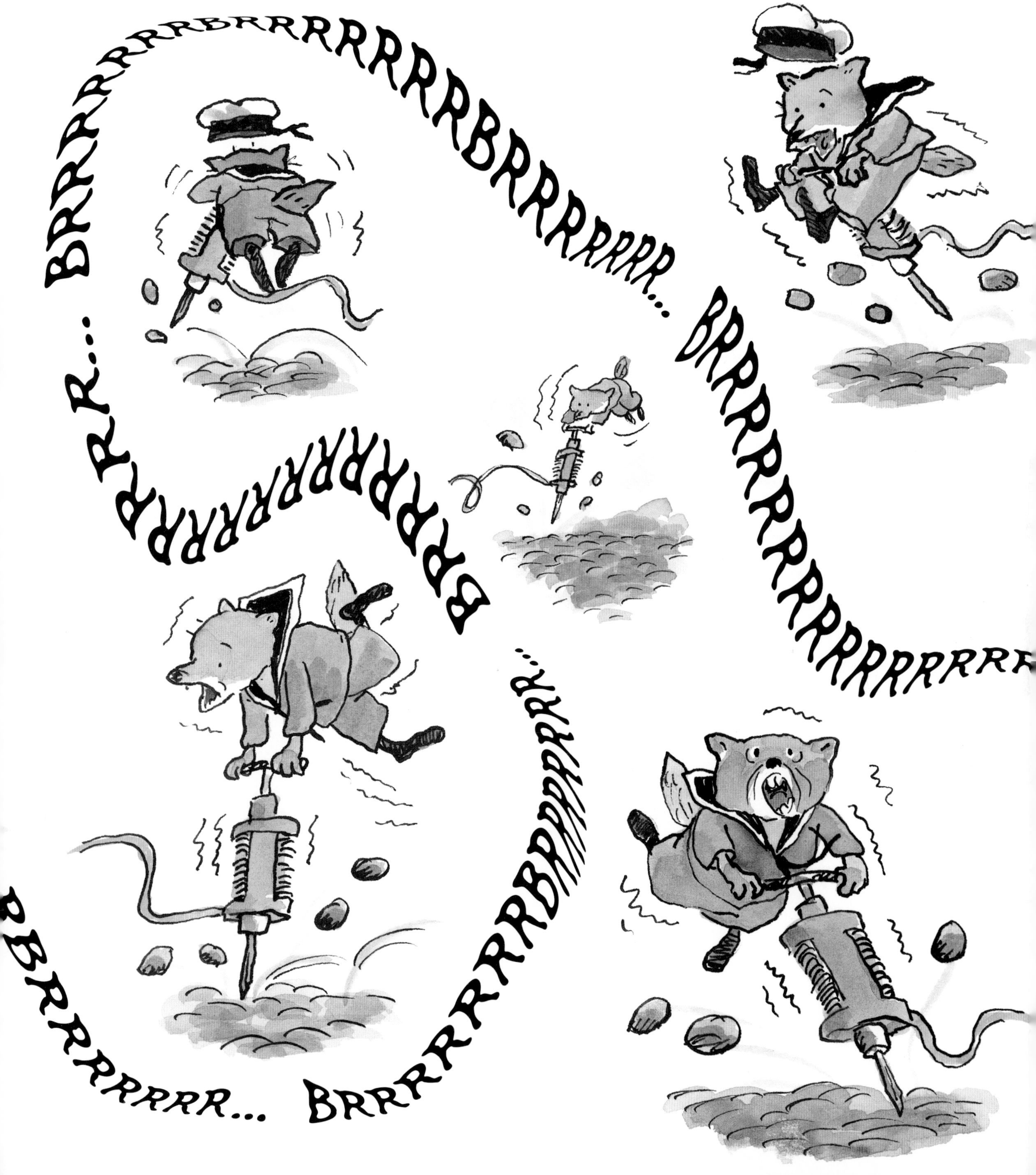

Soon there was a big hole.

"Well done, Smells!" said Mum. "What a clever cub!"

"For your next Badness lesson," said Dad,

"We'll go to the café."

"Ooh, THANKS, Dad!" said Little.

"Gurrr!" said Dad. "Stop being so polite, Little!

Why can't you learn to misbehave?"

At the café, Little tried really hard to be bad. Out went his tongue, wiggle, wiggle. "Poor little cubby, you must be thirsty," said the waitress.

She patted him on the head and gave him a nice cold milk shake.

Smells went screamy-scream, until he got a milk shake too. He gulped it down in one go...

Then he went...

BBBBBBBBUURPPPP!

"Well done, our darling baby pet!"
said Mum and Dad. "That was very bad."

"I will try being bad one more time!" said Little.

He jumped up and went, "Gurrr!"

"Oh, what a lovely smile, little cubby!" said the waitress.

She patted him on the head and gave him a doggy choc.

Smellybreff was getting hungry.
He ate four banana splits and
a knickerbocker glory!

Then he was sick on the floor.
"What a clever cub!"
said Mum.

Along came the waitress, with soapy
water in a bucket, to clean up the mess.
Out went Smellybreff's naughty tail.

WHOOPS!

went the waitress.

"OUT!" shouted the waitress. "Go away, you horrible animals and never-never-never come back!"
She chased them all the way to the bridge.

By then it was getting dark.
There was no Danger sign.
And there were no
warning lights.

"AAH!" went Mum as she tripped on Little Wolf's mud pie.

"WHOAAA!" went Dad as he fell through the hole that Smellybreff had made.

Dad crawled back on to the bridge.
Little said, "Arrroooo! Smellybreff made a nice
big hole in the road. And my mud pie made Mum
slip over and knock you down it, Dad!"

Back at the lair, Little said, "What a lot we learned about Badness today, Mum and Dad! Will you teach me and Smells loads more tomorrow!"

All Mum and Dad could say was

"GURRR!"

So, Little sang this naughty lullaby
to make Mum and Dad feel better:

Hushaby, wolf cub,
Please do not snore –
Or I will shut your
Tail in the door.
Mummy and Daddy
Both need a rest.
Wait till tomorrow –
Then be a pest!